Maggie and Michael Get Dressed

For **Georgie,**
a good pup
2004–2014

Henry Holt and Company, LLC
Publishers since 1866
175 Fifth Avenue, New York, New York 10010
mackids.com

Henry Holt® is a registered trademark of Henry Holt
and Company, LLC.
Copyright © 2016 by Denise Fleming

Library of Congress Cataloging-in-Publication Data
Fleming, Denise, 1950- author, illustrator.
Maggie and Michael get dressed / Denise Fleming. — First edition.
pages   cm
Summary: It is time to get dressed and Michael counts on his dog,
Maggie, for help as he places yellow socks, a brown hat, blue pants,
and other colorful articles of clothing where they belong.
ISBN 978-0-8050-8794-9 (hardback)
[1. Clothing and dress—Fiction. 2. Color—Fiction. 3. Dogs—Fiction.]
I. Title. II. Title: Time to get dressed!
PZ7.F5994Mag 2016   [E]—dc23   2015005807

Henry Holt books may be purchased for business or promotional use.
For information on bulk purchases,
please contact the Macmillan Corporate and Premium
Sales Department at (800) 221-7945 x5442 or by e-mail
at specialmarkets@macmillan.com.

First edition—2016
Printed in China by RR Donnelley Asia Printing Solutions Ltd.,
Dongguan City, Guangdong Province

1   3   5   7   9   10   8   6   4   2

The illustrations were created by pulp painting, a papermaking technique using colored
cotton fiber poured through hand-cut stencils. Accents were added with pastel pencil.
Book design by Denise Fleming and David Powers.

Visit denisefleming.com.

Maggie and Michael Get Dressed

Denise Fleming

Henry Holt and Company ★ New York

Michael,
it's time to get dressed.

Maggie, did you hear that?
It's time to get dressed!

Look, Maggie—socks.
Yellow socks.

Maggie, come back here!

Socks go on your feet,
Maggie,
not in your mouth.

Which shirt, Maggie? The **purple** shirt or the **green** shirt with **orange** stripes?

Over your head, Maggie.
Good girl.

Look, Maggie—pants.
Blue pants with big pockets.

Other end, girl.

Maggie!
Too many kisses!

Black boots or red sneakers?

Brown hat or pink cap?

We forgot underwear,
Maggie!
Look, it's white.

Michael, are you dressed?

Almost!

I'll be back soon, Maggie.
Be a good girl.

Maggie...

I'm home!

Did you miss me, Maggie?

The end.